Taking Depression to School

by Kathy Khalsa, OTR/L

Adapted for the Special Kids in School® series
created by Kim Gosselin

JayJo Books, L.L.C.
Publishing Special Books for Special Kids®

Taking Depression to School

Edited by Karen Schader

Published by
JayJo Books, LLC
A Guidance Channel Company
Publishing Special Books for Special Kids®

JayJo Books is a publisher of books to help teachers, parents, and children cope with chronic illnesses, special needs, and health education in classroom, family, and social settings.

Library of Congress Control Number: 2002108361
ISBN 1-891383-22-1
First Edition
Fourteenth book in our ***Special Kids in School®*** series

For information about
Premium and Special Sales, contact:
JayJo Books Special Sales Office
P.O. Box 213
Valley Park, MO 63088-0213
636-861-1331
jayjobooks@aol.com
www.jayjo.com

For all other information, contact:
JayJo Books
135 Dupont Street, P.O. Box 760
Plainview, NY 11803-0760
1-800-999-6884
jayjobooks@guidancechannel.com
www.jayjo.com

The opinions in this book are solely those of the author. Medical care is highly individualized and should never be altered without professional medical consultation.

Author's Note

This book is dedicated to the hope and belief that all children can be sensitive and understanding about depression.

I would like to thank the people who were so enthusiastic about this project and those who so openly shared their experiences and knowledge of depression in order to help others:

Amy Brodsky
Sandy Browne
Dr. Vera Buk-Bjere
Adam Davis
Arielle Korb

Dr. Penny Frese
Mason Korb
Shayna Livia Korb
Ester Leutenberg
Jay Leutenberg

Anthony Patrick
Xanthe Phillips
Lucy Ritzic
Richard Winder
Michelle Hoffman-Yitzhaki

Hi! My name is Emily. I have childhood depression. You wouldn't know that if I didn't tell you, right? I look the same as other kids. But sometimes, I feel different from other kids.

It took my parents a while to figure out that I needed to go to the doctor. Sometimes I felt very scared, but there was no real reason for me to be scared. Sometimes I felt sad, but there was no real reason for being so sad. I even cried a LOT one day and I didn't know why.

I didn't just feel bad for one day, I felt bad for a while... and I felt bad about myself!

xoxox

In school, I didn't feel like I fit in with the other kids. I had trouble making friends. I had problems thinking about what the teacher was talking about. I had other thoughts in my head...that something bad might happen.

I couldn't even pay attention in science, and I LOVE science!

My dad saw that I wasn't having any fun...doing anything! I didn't feel like climbing my favorite tree. I didn't feel like eating chocolate chip cookies. I didn't even feel like playing computer games. I just wanted to be by myself. He asked me what was wrong, but I couldn't really explain it. I told him my tummy felt bad and I didn't have good thoughts in my head.

I was having trouble talking about how I felt. I just felt really yucky.

My mom and dad took me to a doctor called a psychiatrist (what a big word!). Dr. Vera was very nice. She asked my parents and me a lot of questions. After she listened, she explained that I had childhood depression. Other kids might be sad or in a bad mood for a day or so, and that's okay. But when kids feel really bad for a long time, it's called childhood depression. Dr. Vera explained that both boys and girls could get childhood depression.

She also said I would need to take medicine and talk to a therapist.

Some kids with childhood depression go to a psychiatrist or a therapist. Some kids...like me...go to both. Dr. Vera is a medical doctor, and my therapist David is a psychologist. They both talk to me about how I feel. Dr. Vera talks more about my medicine, and David helps me understand about childhood depression. He helps me learn ways to talk about my feelings and handle them. His office has crayons and toys that I sometimes get to play with. I like that!

I like my psychiatrist and my therapist very much. They both help me live with my depression!

I feel better after seeing Dr. Vera and David. They both told me I am very smart. They also told me it was good that my parents brought me in to get help! They are not really sure how I got childhood depression. I didn't do anything wrong; kids just get it sometimes.

I hope you know that childhood depression isn't contagious. You can't catch it from me or anyone else.

Sometimes I need help remembering to take my medicine. Mom bought me a purple plastic box for my pills. We put it on the kitchen counter to remind us that I need to take them. My parents also help me talk about things, so I won't keep my feelings inside. We talk about ways I can help myself, like resting, getting organized, and talking to my teacher if I need to. We talk about ways to manage my anger so I won't lose control.

Mom and Dad promised that if I'm sad and want to talk, they will always find time to listen.

M T W Th F

I feel much better when I take my medicine. I'm learning to talk about how I feel and what I should do when I feel bad. Sometimes, my feelings are huge and scary...like the whole world is going to crash...and I feel so little and weak. I sure don't like feeling that way!

My therapist works with me on helping me not feel scared and angry. David is teaching me different ways to feel good. He reminds me that I need to get out of bed, even when I don't feel like it! He says I need to control my anger, even when I feel like I can't.

I'm learning to figure out how I feel, and then tell others how I feel too. That sounds a lot easier than it is!

ANGRY
GUILTY
SCARED
SAD
BAD

I worry that if other kids know I go to a psychiatrist and a therapist, they won't like me. They might think I'm crazy or bad. I think that if they know I take medicine, they won't want to be my friends. But then, I know a lot of kids who take medicine, and it's no big deal.

I remember that it's my job to live with my depression the best I can.

What can you do to help me? You can be my friend. I need friends, too, just like everyone else. I might sound angry when I speak to you...but I don't mean to. I might look like I don't want to be with anyone. Some days, I have thoughts that make me sad or worried. I don't want to feel sad or worried, and I try not to. I don't want to be in a bad mood all the time. Just remind me that it'll be okay and that I'll feel better soon. And ask me if I need a hug. I usually do!

Most days, I feel just fine. I like to climb trees, eat chocolate chip cookies and play computer games. Too bad I can't do them all at the same time!

When I grow up, I may still have depression. If I do, I'll sure know how to live with it. When I'm bigger, I want to help people understand depression. A lot of people don't understand it at all! I didn't either, at first. Maybe I'll speak to big groups of people about it. Maybe I'll write another book about it.

I'll decide that later. Right now, I'm going outside to play!

XOXOX

LET'S TAKE THE DEPRESSION KIDS' QUIZ!

1. **If you feel sad for a few minutes, do you have childhood depression?**
   No, childhood depression is a term doctors use when a child has been depressed for a long time.

2. **Does something sad or really bad have to happen for a child to get childhood depression?**
   Not always. Sometimes depression just happens and no one seems to know why.

3. **What does the word "psychiatrist" mean?**
   A psychiatrist is a medical doctor who knows a lot about the way kids act and feel. Psychiatrists can help you get medications if you need them.

4. **What does a therapist do?**
   A therapist teaches you different ways to help you feel better, if you are feeling sad or having other feelings you need help with.

5. **If you're feeling really bad or sad or having unhealthy thoughts, what should you do?**
   Talk to a trusted adult or friend who will listen.

6. **You can tell which kids have childhood depression just by looking at them. True or false?**
   False. You can't tell *just* by looking at them.

7. **What might be signs of childhood depression?**
   a. not wanting to get out of bed for a long time
   b. not wanting to eat favorite foods or play with favorite toys for days
   c. thinking bad things about yourself
   d. feeling sad or grouchy a lot
   e. not thinking right in school
   f. all of the above

8. **Is childhood depression contagious?**
   No, you can't catch it from anyone.

9. **What can you do to help someone with childhood depression?**
   Listen and be a good friend.

10. **People who have childhood depression...**
    a. will definitely have it when they are grown-up.
    b. will definitely not have it when they are grown-up.
    c. We really don't know if they will have it as adults.
    (But we do know that if children get treated for depression and they do have it as adults, they will have an easier time managing it!)

Great job! Thanks for taking the Depression Kids' Quiz!

TEN TIPS FOR TEACHERS

1.RECOGNIZING AND UNDERSTANDING CHILDHOOD DEPRESSION CAN BE TRICKY.

Depression doesn't ALWAYS appear the same in every child. Noticing the signs of childhood depression can be difficult, as they are seen in a wide variety of behaviors. Some students may exhibit no acting-out behaviors and appear socially withdrawn. Some children may be highly irritable and angry. Specialists like school nurses, school counselors, and psychologists may be good resources if you have concerns about a child.

2. BE AWARE OF THE REFERRAL SYSTEM.

Children living with childhood depression are often not referred for help and are underserved. By knowing the system in your school, you may be able to advocate for a child.

3. CONSIDER BEHAVIORS AS SYMPTOMS, NOT ATTENTION-SEEKING.

Viewing behaviors like restlessness, irritability, crying, social withdrawing, and sadness as related to childhood depression—as opposed to the child not behaving—may be helpful for both you and the child.

4. SEE STRENGTHS.

Often, students who live with depression don't see themselves as valuable. Finding and pointing out their natural strengths is a way to allow them to feel successful.

5. PARENTS AND TEACHERS CAN BE TEAM MEMBERS!

Parents may offer valuable input about how sleep, eating habits, stress, and other factors might affect classroom learning. Being in contact with and including parents can be beneficial to all! And input from a teacher's observation about social interaction, energy level, and motivation can be extremely useful to the parents as well.

6. BE PROACTIVE.

If a child is struggling, go the extra mile to make him or her feel special. Do not allow them to be left out when children are working in pairs; assign partners instead. If a job is done well, feel free to offer praise. Kids who live with childhood depression may be especially receptive to hearing well-deserved positives about their accomplishments.

7. DEPRESSION IS NOT CONTAGIOUS.

Even if a child with depression talks about his or her feelings to another child, the listener won't necessarily get depressed. Facilitating friendships and good listening skills is valuable for all kids.

8. BE AWARE OF SIDE EFFECTS.

If you know a child is on medications, it may be helpful to know the side effects, so that you know what to watch for and report. This information may be available from the person who notified you that the child is taking medications.

9. EDUCATE TO EMPOWER.

Childhood depression is commonly misunderstood and may even have a stigma associated with it. Comments like, "He's so young, what does he have to be depressed about?" perpetuate a lack of understanding. Set the stage for accurate education with up-to-date books, curriculums, or speakers.

10. EXPECT GOOD DAYS AND BAD DAYS.

Even a kid who is stabilized on effective medication and working with a great therapist may have some difficult days. Accepting this may help to reduce stress for the child and the teacher.

ADDITIONAL RESOURCES

Center for Mental Health Services
Knowledge Exchange Network
PO BOX 42490
Washington, DC 20015
1-800-789-2647
www.mentalhealth.org

Depression and Related Affective Disorders Association (DRADA)
Meyer 3-181
600 North Wolfe Street
Baltimore, MD 21287-7381
1-410-955-4647
www.drada.org

National Alliance for the Mentally Ill
200 N. Glebe Road
Suite 1015
Arlington, VA 22203-3754
1-800-950-6264
www.nami.org

Federation of Families for Children's Mental Health
1101 King Street Suite 420
Alexandria, VA 22314
1-703-684-7710
www.ffcmh.org

American Academy of Child and Adolescent Psychiatry
3615 Wisconsin Avenue, N. W.
Washington DC 20016
1-800-333-7636
www.aacap.org

National Mental Health Association
2001 N. Beauregard Street, 12th Floor
Alexandria, VA 22311
1-800-969-6642
www.nmha.org

To order additional copies of Taking Depression to School or inquire about our quantity discounts for schools, hospitals, and affiliated organizations, contact us at 1-800-999-6884.

From our *Special Kids in School®* series

Taking A.D.D. to School
Taking Arthritis to School
Taking Asthma to School
Taking Autism to School
Taking Cancer to School
Taking Cerebral Palsy to School
Taking Cystic Fibrosis to School
Taking Diabetes to School
Taking Down Syndrome to School
Taking Dyslexia to School
Taking Food Allergies to School
Taking Seizure Disorders to School
Taking Tourette Syndrome to School
...and others coming soon!

From our new *Healthy Habits for Kids®* series

There's a Louse in My House
A Fun Story about Kids and Head Lice

From our new *Special Family and Friends™* series

Allie Learns About Alzheimer's Disease
A Family Story about Love, Patience, and Acceptance
Patrick Learns About Parkinson's Disease
A Story of a Special Bond Between Friends
... and others coming soon!

And from our *Substance Free Kids®* series

Smoking STINKS!!™
A Heartwarming Story about the Importance of Avoiding Tobacco

Other books available now!

SPORTSercise!
A School Story about Exercise-Induced Asthma
ZooAllergy
A Fun Story about Allergy and Asthma Triggers
Rufus Comes Home
Rufus the Bear with Diabetes™
A Story about Diagnosis and Acceptance
The ABC's of Asthma
An Asthma Alphabet Book for Kids of All Ages
Taming the Diabetes Dragon
A Story about Living Better with Diabetes
Trick-or-Treat for Diabetes
A Halloween Story for Kids Living with Diabetes

A portion of the proceeds from all our publications is donated to various charities to help fund important medical research and education. We work hard to make a difference in the lives of children with chronic conditions and/or special needs. Thank you for your support.

XOXOX